# MARVEL™

# THE AMAZING® SPIDER-MAN

# PICTURE PERFECT

Read along as Spider-Man tangles with the Green Goblin. You will know it is time to turn the page when you hear this sound.... Ready? Let's begin!

**publications international, ltd.**

W9-ARV-436

"Parker!" J. Jonah Jameson's voice booms through *The Daily Bugle* office. Mr. Jameson marches towards Peter Parker. "You call these pictures? I want pictures of that troublemaker Spider-Man! You have until 5:00 today!"

Peter sighs. "I'll see what I can do, Mr. Jameson."

"If you don't get me pictures of that web-head, you'll be seeing what you can do about a new job!"

"Sure thing, Mr. Jameson—" Peter says. J. Jonah Jameson slams his office door and cuts off Peter before he finishes speaking.

Peter knows he can't afford to lose the money he makes taking pictures for the newspaper.

As he tries to decide what to do, he sees two street thugs steal a purse from an old lady. They start playing catch with the purse, throwing it just out of her reach.

"Looks like I'll be pulling double-duty on this one," Peter says to himself. "Time for your friendly neighborhood Spider-Man... and photographer!"

Then he ducks behind a building to change into Spider-Man.

The purse flies through the air, just past the old lady's fingers. One thug reaches up to grab it. Before he can touch it, Spider-Man swings by and grabs the purse out of the air.

"Here you go, ma'am," Spider-Man says as he hands the purse back to the lady.

The two thugs turn to run away. Spider-Man shoots his web and catches them. He wraps them tightly in his web and points to a camera hanging from a gutter.

"Smile, boys! You'll be on the front page tomorrow!"
Spider-Man waves to the camera to set off the motion sensor,
and the camera flashes.

Police cars speed up as Spider-Man jumps on a wall.
"You two jokers didn't get far after escaping from jail," one of the police officers says as he puts the thugs in his car. "Back to prison with you."

"Well, they did look a little homesick," Spider-Man says to himself as he looks on.

Suddenly an explosion rips the air. And right after, Spider-Man hears a familiar cackle.

The Green Goblin zooms above the street on his glider and stops over a wrecked police car. The back doors of the car open, and a crook climbs out. As smoke clogs the air, police officers point at the Green Goblin hovering above them. The Green Goblin tosses his pumpkin bombs and laughs his evil laugh.

"I'll keep releasing criminals until that wall-crawler shows up!"

11

Spider-Man arrives on the scene just as the Green Goblin starts to zoom away. Spider-Man slings his camera across his back and shoots a web to catch the Goblin's glider.

As he looks down on the city streets far below, Spider-Man thinks that if he can get a picture of Spider-Man capturing the Green Goblin, J. Jonah Jameson won't threaten to fire Peter again.

The Green Goblin looks over his shoulder and sees Spider-Man. "You!" the Green Goblin screams. Then he plunges toward the streets below, trying to shake Spider-Man from his web.

Spider-Man falls into a trash bin. Shortly after, the Green Goblin comes gliding in.

"Come out, come out, wherever you are," he says.

"Say cheese!" Spider-Man says as the camera's flash goes off. The Goblin is briefly blinded. Spider-Man tackles him.

As they fight, the camera's special motion sensor snaps pictures. Then the Goblin jumps at Spider-Man, grabs his mask, and pulls.

Spider-Man's mask comes off! The camera flashes before Spider-Man is able to put it back on.

The Green Goblin cackles, knocks Spider-Man to the ground, grabs the camera, and zooms away.

Spider-Man gets up, but the Green Goblin is gone. "I have to get that camera back!" he says. He calls *The Daily Bugle*. He tells Mr. Jameson that he has some pictures of Spider-Man fighting the Green Goblin, but he won't be able to get them to the paper until later.

"Too late, Parker!" J. Jonah barks into the phone. "The Green Goblin left a message saying he has a big picture for me—a picture of Spider-Man's secret identity! I'm just waiting to hear where to meet him."

Spider-Man hangs up the phone and makes his way to the *Daily Bugle* office.

A phone rings in the quiet *Daily Bugle* office. "This is Jameson!" J. Jonah says when he answers. He pauses and listens. "Yes, I know exactly where that is. I'll meet you there in half an hour. And listen, Goblin, this better not be some kind of trick—hello? Hello?"

Spider-Man clings to the wall outside Mr. Jameson's office. When Mr. Jameson leaves the building to meet the Goblin, Spider-Man follows.

The lights are very dim on the deserted dock where J. Jonah Jameson meets the Green Goblin.

"Let's get this over with, Goblin," J. Jonah says.

"Soon the world will know who Spider-Man really is!" the Green Goblin says as he hands the camera to J. Jonah.

Suddenly a web shoots down and grabs the camera.

"Spider-Man!" J. Jonah shouts.

"Give that back to me!" the Green Goblin shrieks.

"Finders keepers, losers weepers," Spider-Man laughs.

Then the Green Goblin leaps at Spider-Man.

The camera drops from Spider-Man's hands. Spider-Man and the Green Goblin battle, but neither one can defeat the other. Finally the Goblin knocks a pile of crates toward Spider-Man. Spider-Man rolls and grabs the camera before any crates land on it.

J. Jonah Jameson has been hiding from the fight. When the crates fall, he bolts down the street. Spider-Man secretly snaps a shot of Mr. Jameson as he runs away.

The Goblin tries to escape too. But Spider-Man quickly wraps him in a web and leaves him for the police.

"Love to chat, Gobby, but I have some business to take care of."

The next day at *The Daily Bugle*, Peter walks into Mr. Jameson's office. Mr. Jameson holds an envelope in his hands. The words "Photo of the True Identity of Spider-Man" are written on the envelope.

As Mr. Jameson tears open the envelope, he says, "Tomorrow's headline will read 'Spider-Menace Identity Revealed!' and this will be the full-page picture!" Then he takes out the picture and holds it up.

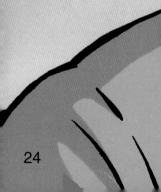